P9-BYO-498

Judge Benjamin:
THE
SUPERDOG
SURPRISE

Weekly Reader Books presents

Judge Benjamin:
THE
SUPERDOG
SURPRISE

Judith Whitelock McInerney

DRAWINGS BY *Leslie Morrill*

HOLIDAY HOUSE
NEW YORK

This book is a presentation of Weekly Reader Books.
Weekly Reader Books offers book clubs for children from
preschool through high school.

For further information write to:
Weekly Reader Books
4343 Equity Drive
Columbus, Ohio 43228

Library of Congress Cataloging in Publication Data

McInerney, Judith Whitelock.
Judge Benjamin, the superdog surprise.

Summary: Judge Benjamin, a St. Bernard, solves a
mystery while stranded with "his" family in an abandoned
farmhouse during a blizzard.
1. Children's stories, American. [1. St. Bernard
dogs—Fiction. 2. Dogs—Fiction. 3. Humorous stories]
I. Morrill, Leslie H., ill. II. Title.
PZ7.M47865Jvb 1985   [Fic]   84–48745
ISBN 0-8234-0561-3

Edited for Weekly Reader Books and published by arrangement with Holiday House.

for MARTY—
and her Sainted crew

Judge Benjamin:
THE
SUPERDOG
SURPRISE

Chapter 1

Car trouble was the last thing we needed.

My paw had fallen asleep under the weight of little Annie in the back of the O'Riley station wagon. When I tried to gently shift positions, I saw the red oil light flashing the bad news on the dashboard. We were on our way home from Metropolis, where we'd been helping out on Great-Gramps's farm. Decatur was still hours away.

I don't know too many St. Bernards who are mechanical geniuses. I'm certainly not one of them—Judge Benjamin O'Riley, family St. Bernard who specializes in loving that family. But I figured the car was trying to tell us something and it probably wasn't good news.

4   JUDGE BENJAMIN:

"Maggie, we'll have to pull off in Sandoval," Tom said softly so he wouldn't wake the four sleeping children. "I just put oil in at the last gas stop. Something must be wrong."

Maggie reached behind her to adjust Maura in her car seat and to glance at the sleeping Annie. Maggie didn't approve of riding without seat belts, but since Annie always wriggled out when she slept, Maggie had given in and let her lie in the far back of the wagon with me.

"Surely, it can't be too serious," she said. "You just took this car in for a tune-up last month."

The look on Tom's face gave him away. He hadn't quite made that appointment.

Maggie's voice rose past a whisper. "Didn't you?"

One by one the O'Riley children—Seth, Kathleen, Annie, and little Maura—stirred.

"What's the matter?" Seth asked. "Are we stopping to eat?"

A typical Seth remark. That growing boy could put away food almost as well as I could.

Annie yawned and sat up, rubbing her eyes with the hand that was still holding my ear.

"You'll have to come up here and put your shoulder harness on. I know better than to trust you to stay still," Kathleen said, reaching back and pulling Annie to a spot in the middle of the seat with her.

It gave me a little room to stretch.

Kathleen fumbled with Annie's buckle. Then she asked Tom, "What's wrong anyway? I could have slept clear through to Decatur if Seth hadn't gotten noisy."

Seth shrugged his shoulders. "I didn't break the car. I just asked about it."

"Cin we Elmer's-Glue it?" Annie was still yawning.

Elmer's Glue was Annie's solution to just about everything. She tried to glue raisins on a peanut butter sandwich once. Even I wouldn't touch that one.

By the time Tom pulled in at the Sandoval gas station, a favorite stop for truckers with its nearby restaurant, the red light had stopped flashing. It simply glowed steadily red.

"We can get a bite next door while the mechanic has a look," Tom said. "It's about break time anyway."

"You have only one shoe, Annie. You can't go out like that. It's raining." Kathleen was crawling on the floor, looking for the other sneaker.

"Wrong, Kathleen. Those are snowflakes, not rain," Seth said. He never missed a chance to correct Kathleen. There weren't too many times when he had the opportunity, so he made the most of it now.

"Mom, he's right. Those flakes are getting really fat." Kathleen had come up from the floor for a better look at the weather.

"Here it is, Annie. It got pushed under the seat up front." Maggie handed the shoe back. "What else are we missing before we disembark?"

"Wot's barking? Judge isn't barking. Wot you mean, Mommy?" Annie stuck her untied sneaker toward the front, waiting for someone to help.

"It means get out of the car, Annie. Now. I'm starved." Seth opened the door and was on his way into the restaurant.

Tom stopped him. "Not so fast. Best take the Judge for a walk to stretch his legs."

Seth's stomach growled and he looked glum, but he didn't complain.

Maggie and the girls went inside the restaurant while Tom went to talk to the mechanic. Then Tom joined the rest of the family inside.

Seth and I moseyed around a bit.

The snowflakes were indeed getting much bigger. I had to keep blinking to see.

We noticed a NO PETS sign on the door to the restaurant.

I suspected as much.

"Don't worry, Judge. We'll sneak something out to you." Seth brushed some of the snow from my nose. "Do you want to wait in the car or out here?"

I noticed another car riding up on one of those hydraulic lifts in the gas station bay. I decided I preferred my four paws on the ground.

I sat down.

"Okay, big fella." Seth put my leash around a limb of a small tree, more to show the world that I was corralled than anything else. Seth knew it wouldn't have held a frog, let alone two hundred pounds of big dog. "How do two double cheese-burgers sound? Or maybe a barbecue?"

I wasn't sure if he was reciting the menu for me or for him, but either way, both sounded good.

I huddled under the roof at the edge of the building. That plus the shelter of the tree offered good protection from the wet, falling snow. Everything from my neck back stayed fairly dry. My face wouldn't have gotten such a brush of white if I weren't so nosy. I stuck my face into the storm so I could watch everyone who approached the restaurant.

This place was as good as a bus station for people watching.

Chapter 2

The weather played games, first soft and fluffy snow, then wet, freezing rain, finally back to soft and fluffy again. It was beginning to stick, and the combination would make driving treacherous.

Every few minutes another car would pull in at the little restaurant.

A tall, bearded man in a pickup raced in to fill two big coffee thermoses. In the few minutes needed for this errand, his car became buried in icy white. He made a second trip inside to buy a new scraper after his broke. Coming out, he handed me one of two Milky Ways. It was the first in a parade of handouts.

"Came up pretty fast, didn't it, big fella?" he said. "Not a clue in yesterday's forecast either."

I nodded. We'd had the radio on all the way from Metropolis, and the weatherman forecast only gusty winds and shower activity.

The man brushed some of the snow from my head. Real friendly guy, he was.

"Hope I can make it to Chicago before they start closing roads." He headed back to his pickup for one more scrape job.

Closing the roads? The snow just started! It couldn't get that bad that fast.

But I know never to underestimate Mother Nature.

An old Chevrolet with rusting sides nearly rolled into the corner of the brick building. The driver got out of the car and spoke loudly through the windshield. She was a heavyset woman with orange hair and a bright red stocking cap. She wore hiking boots and new blue jeans.

"Maude, get out here. You gotta go look at this statue."

She was staring at me.

Statue? I stood up and sat down again, but she was brushing snow from her horn-rimmed glasses and missed the action.

"Hurry up, Maude. It's the last one and it's just what we need between our pink flamingos. Maybe we can buy it cheap."

Maude, on the passenger side, was taking her sweet time.

Two legs dangled from the open door. Pretty soon, two gloved hands holding Reindeer plastic boots joined them. I could tell it was decision time: boots over patent leather pumps? Pumps off, then boots? Should she put her boots on while still wearing those gloves?

The restaurant door banged open and Kathleen appeared, coatless. "Here, Judge. I didn't forget you." She shoveled a handful of french fries into my mouth. "They think I'm in the bathroom." She patted my ear and then raced inside.

"Never mind, Maude. It's not for sale," the driver said as she watched me chew and swallow. She pulled a package of Life Savers from her coat pocket and handed me one.

Hmm. Peppermint with a real bite. And just a little fuzzy lint.

Maude finally made it out of the car. She had kept her gloves on, so she couldn't fasten the boot snaps, and they flapped noisily as she stomped toward us.

"I declare, Gertie. I didn't know they made dogs that big," Maude said.

I decided to take that as a compliment. In a moment of uncontrolled arrogance, I stood up, puffed out my chest, and barked gratefully.

The boots weren't a handicap at all. Maude and Gertie must have been marathoners. Those ladies *zoomed* inside.

I guess I overstated my gratitude.

Seth came out next with two double cheese-burgers.

"I forgot the ketchup," he apologized. "Annie was making a fort with the bottles on the table. I hope it's okay." He unwrapped the sandwiches, watched me wolf them down, then headed back inside.

No sooner was Seth gone than Tom came out. He handed me a barbecue. "Hope Annie didn't get carried away with the hot sauce," he said on his way to chat with the mechanic. "She took charge of all the bottles."

She had. It was good but sooooo tangy. I sat there with my tongue hanging out, hoping to catch the snow to put out the blaze.

The people in the restaurant looked out the window and mistook my wide-open mouth as a sign of hunger. There was a run on doggy bags, all for me.

Absolutely everyone gave me food.

Eating it caused me a few problems.

Besides barbecue, Mexican recipes were a very hot number on the restaurant's menu.

I say *verrrrry* hot.

The more tacos, enchiladas, and tamales I ate, the more my smoldering throat screamed for a bucket of water.

The wind had picked up and so had the snow. Tom and Maggie went together to check on the car, leaving the kids to linger over their desserts.

That's when Annie made a move.

She put on her coat and trounced up to the counter, climbing on top of one of those rotating stools.

I could see her shaking her finger at the waitress, the lady with a puffy hair style and striped pink uniform who had handed out doggy bags. The more excited Annie got, the more the stool turned. Annie pointed her finger to the sign on the door with such energy that she nearly went sailing.

The waitress finally grabbed her by the waist, hoisted her to the door, and handed her the NO PETS sign. Together they scribbled:

EXCEPT IN A SNOWSTORM.

Annie grabbed my leash and led me inside.

I don't know whether that waitress smelled my burrito breath or just had an instinct for kindness. She brought me to a back storeroom. There she pulled a clean dishpan from a shelf and filled it with good, cold milk.

Aaaaah. Nothing, but nothing, works as well for washing food down.

She had made a friend for life.

Chapter 3

I was drinking my third quart when Maggie and Tom came back with news. The storeroom overlooked the dining area, and the O'Riley table stood just a few feet away. Annie kept pitching french fries over the threshold to me. Several landed in my milk.

"You may as well order another dessert, Seth," Maggie said.

"It's an oil gasket," Tom explained. "It'll be another half-hour, maybe more. That mechanic moves at two speeds: slow and very slow."

"Dad, the snow is really coming down," Kathleen said. "If we have to wait much longer . . ."

"Don't be a fuddy-duddy, Kathleen. We've

driven in snow before." Seth ordered another piece of lemon pie. It looked pretty good, but I was too full to beg. Besides, I was worried about the snow, too, and for once, food took second place in my thoughts.

"What's a fud-dud?" Annie was sneaking meringue with her finger. I expected her to flip the sweet white goo into my milk next. "Why do you awways use big words like dat?" she asked.

The waitress—her name tag read TRIXIE LEE —refilled Seth's milk. "Fuddy-duddy is a kind of made-up word, hon," Trixie Lee explained to Annie. "Something like nanny-nanny boo-boo. You can make it mean a lot of things."

Annie was instantly satisfied. That waitress was toddler-lingual.

"Does look pretty bad out, though," she went on. "Seen these storms sneak up awful fast and close highways."

The waitress was the second person to mention the threat of closed roads. I didn't like it. I could tell by Tom's frown that it made him uneasy, too.

"It's lucky the leaky gasket is on top of the motor," he said, "or we'd be spending the night in Sandoval."

"Not much chance of that," Trixie said. "Folks

already filled up the only rooms in town. Lookee there."

She pointed to the NO VACANCY sign in bright red neon glowing at the motel across the road.

Maggie looked at the sign, the snow, and then Tom.

The snow was really coming down.

Any other time we would have been making the trip in the camper and it wouldn't have been a problem. We could have just pulled into a rest stop and waited it out. But Tom had sent the glaziers from his business to a new job site in the Pace Arrow after they had helped rebuild Great-Gramps's barn. We were making do with the station wagon.

Tom made yet another trip to the gas station.

I suppose he figured the guy could be hurried in light of the bad weather.

Maggie ordered more hot tea, and Kathleen played Old Maid with Annie.

Maura, stuffed with crackers dipped in applesauce, had fallen asleep in the highchair.

Seth was eating pretzels.

We were the only customers left.

Trixie Lee sat down to chat.

"You know, I could put you folks up," she said. "My place is just a three-roomer, but heck, I'm used to roughing it. I took Joe's five kids once," she said, pointing over toward the gas station at the mechanic, "and we managed for two crowded weeks."

"Nice of you," Maggie said, smiling. "But there are lots more motels along the way. If it gets too bad, we'll find a place. To tell the truth, we're just awfully anxious to make it back to Decatur. We've been away longer than we ever intended."

Maggie told the waitress about our extended stay in Metropolis with Great-Gramps. It was nervous chatter. Somehow the silent snow seemed louder than their words.

The wind had picked up.

Not a good sign—drifting was the most dangerous of snow problems.

When Tom finally came back in to announce that the car was indeed ready, he carried two extra flashlights and two thermoses he had purchased from the garage. Trixie Lee filled one with coffee and one with hot chocolate. She stuffed several packages of peanut butter crackers and Oreo cookies in Seth's pockets and wished us luck. She handed Kathleen a battered aluminum pie tin.

"Make sure that big fella gets enough water,

you hear? Melted snow will do him just fine."
Trixie Lee winked at me.

Snow would never taste as refreshing as
Trixie's dishpan full of milk, but then what
would?

Tom paid the bill. It wasn't nearly as large as
he expected, what with my milk and Seth's over-
time appetite. I noticed he left a generous tip,
and I was glad.

"We should be able to get as far as Salem anyway," he said when we'd gotten into the car.
"According to the radio, the storm hasn't started
there yet. Salem has several nice motels, and I
doubt they'll all be full."

Maggie nodded but couldn't hide a frown. She
checked to see that everyone was buckled up,
and Tom started the car.

"The mechanic offered to put us up at his
house," Tom said.

"So did Trixie Lee," Maggie answered. "Nice
small-town people, aren't they? But I didn't have
the heart to inflict six O'Rileys and a St. Bernard
on any stranger overnight!"

She was trying to make a joke, but it sounded
hollow.

Maggie was right, though. We would have
been a crowd any way you looked at it.

Tom drove very slowly, the windshield wipers barely keeping up with the thick flakes.

Fewer and fewer cars were on the highway. The center line became impossible to see.

Maggie adjusted the radio to keep posted on the forecast.

It kept getting worse.

Bad as it was, there didn't seem to be anything to gain by turning back.

We just forged ahead.

In one hour we only managed to cover twenty-one miles.

Maura and Annie both fell asleep, unaware of the danger of the growing blizzard outside.

No one had much to say.

Three times Tom had to stop, put his flashers on, and clean off snow that had gathered in the middle of the windshield between the wipers, and on the back glass.

Each time, we held our breath. A car coming from behind could have hit us so easily.

But no one was coming from behind.

For that matter, no one was going.

No one, that is, except the O'Rileys.

Until . . . until we hit the snowbank . . .

Chapter 4

It happened eight miles shy of Salem.

It wasn't a crash. We were creeping along at twelve miles an hour. It was a dull thud.

Part of that was me.

My ribs collided with the back of the seat. Thank heavens everyone else was wearing a seat belt. I heard the crunching crackers in Seth's pocket when my paw flew over the seat in front of me. The smell of peanut butter oozed from the corduroy.

"Everyone okay?" Tom yelled.

A chorus of yesses echoed through the car.

"Did we go off the road?" Maggie was checking Maura, who had started to giggle just as the bang awoke her. She must have been having some funny dream.

"No. More like the road came to meet us," Tom answered. "We've hit a drift. I'll get out and take a look."

"Don't worry, kids. We have the trouble shovel in the back. We'll be on track real soon." Maggie's reassurance was only half convincing. The entire hood of the car had slipped beneath the white powder. Digging out would be no small matter.

Tom came to the back of the station wagon and let me out. "I can use an extra set of paws, my friend," he told me.

I was glad he asked. I intended to make my Swiss ancestors proud.

Tom took a moment to check me over. He felt my ribs and legs slowly. "Good stock, huh, Judge? Nothing broken on this hulk." He patted my head.

The snowy roadblock was as high as my shoulder and a whole lot thicker. I made a gradual dent in it by charging back and forth in front of the car as Tom directed so he could see to dig out the wheels.

We worked for half an hour, then got back into the car, started the engine, and tried to warm up a bit.

"I'll take a shift, Dad," Seth volunteered.

"Me, too," Kathleen offered.

"Don't forget me," Maggie added. "I've had plenty of practice with your winter trips, Tom."

Maggie didn't wait for Tom to agree. She got out and started scooping.

It was hard work, but with all of us—even Annie insisted on putting her two cents in—we finally got the car going again.

Unfortunately, again was only twenty feet farther.

Bang. Another drift.

It was discouraging to say the least.

We took turns shoveling again.

The wind was howling, whirling snow around and making it hard to see.

Tom sent everyone back into the car but me.

"Judge, I've got a bad feeling about this," he said. "If these drifts are just the beginning, we'll never make it into Salem."

Tom seldom sounded so pessimistic.

"Let's walk a bit and see."

We stayed close together. Even a St. Bernard does not go out alone in a blizzard. Within six

feet more of clear road, we found another drift.

I strained to see as far as I could. I was sure Tom was right. There were no barriers to prevent drifting—snow fences, shrubs, even trees were scarce in this part of southern central Illinois. Chances were excellent that the entire rural portion of Route 51 was affected.

The wind was really ringing in our ears, and my nose began to sting with the cold.

Frostbite wasn't something to mess around with, and I knew Tom was worried. We couldn't stay out in this snowstorm long without suffering the consequences.

Still, I would have been willing to risk it. Help could be close by, and I was the most qualified to look.

Tom read my mind. "This isn't a night for man or beast to be out, big fella," he said. "I wouldn't want to lose you."

We got back in the car. Before Tom could say a thing, Maggie put a finger to her lips to quiet everyone so we could hear the radio announcer.

"In the worst unanticipated blizzard of this century, central Illinois and southeast Missouri have been inundated with blowing and drifting snow that started early this evening. . . ."

His description went on for several minutes. We didn't have to be told. We were sitting in the middle of it. But his last words were the final blow.

". . . All north-south highways have been officially closed. Plows cannot, we repeat, *cannot* keep up with the downpour and have been called in until morning. . . ."

There was more, and it was all bad. Tom turned the radio off. "Hmmm, folks, this looks like a good place for a picnic," he said, trying to smile.

Maggie pinched her chin between her thumb and forefinger when her lip started to tremble. For everyone's sake she managed a smile.

"Could be good," Maggie said. "No ants."

"Picnic? Oh, goodee!" Annie clapped. "Cin we hab fry chicken?"

"This is going to be a small-scale picnic, dear," Maggie told her. "Kind of snack size. Everybody look through your pockets and see what you can contribute."

While the back-seat people were busy doing that, Maggie whispered to Tom, "What do we do, Tom? We could freeze out here."

"I filled up the tank at Sandoval. As long as I

check the exhaust and crack the windows, we'll be able to run the engine often enough to keep warm," Tom said.

"So long as we keep moving," Maggie said thoughtfully. "Circulation is a key to body heat."

"I've got a couple of flares," Tom went on. "It won't hurt to use them. Somebody could be close enough to notice."

"Why don't you unload the suitcases? The clothes, even the dirty clothes bag—we can make layers of blankets that way," Maggie said softly.

"Good idea," Tom said.

"And Tom, there's a box of candles behind the spare tire. We can use those to melt the snow for water in Trixie Lee's pan," Maggie finished.

"You've been reading those survival magazines again, kiddo." Tom grinned.

"No." Maggie chuckled. "I picked up those candles to deliver to the church. I just never got around to it."

"By morning we should see a snowplow. Or when the sun comes up, we might see a house that's close enough for us to reach with the Judge," Tom said.

Great. I like nothing better than to be useful.

Tom and I got out one more time to find the

things Maggie wanted and to start the flares. Tom planned to set one off every hour as long as they lasted. I stood by the open door blocking some of the wind from blasting inside on the rest of the family.

When everything was passed in to Maggie, Tom went to the front of the car to light the first flare. It made a strange whistling sound, and I jumped.

I turned from the brightness and looked away from the car.

I had the most uncanny feeling that someone was watching me.

For a crazy minute I could have sworn I saw a shadow, not unlike mine, pass through the snow.

What was it?

Imagination does strange things.

Tom opened the door at the back of the car to let me in. I hesitated. Something was there! I didn't just feel the eyes, I saw them.

"Hurry up, fella, we don't want to let any more cold air in the car than we have to," he said, giving me a nudge.

When I got back inside, I took one more long look out the window. I could see nothing, but I had the funniest feeling. . . .

"We've got quite a haul." Maggie interrupted my wild thoughts.

The family food search had turned up a marvelous little assortment of treats.

We had mashed peanut butter crackers.

Annie made herself very useful by picking out the pieces of fluff that frosted them. Whatever had made its home in Seth's pocket had left its nest.

The Oreos survived. Enough for two apiece. I would remember Trixie Lee forever.

Kathleen contributed a half bag of Cheetos and two packs of grape Bubble Yum.

Maggie had butterscotch and mints galore, the usual goodies she kept in the hidden pockets of her travel tote.

Even little Maura had jelly beans in her parka.

Tom found stale potato chips and two Milky Ways in the glove compartment.

And dear sweet Grammy, who never let us leave Metropolis empty-handed, had packed six ham sandwiches "just in case we didn't get a chance to stop."

The only thing missing was green vegetables.

Annie and I both yay-yayed that!

Chapter 5

Maggie and Tom never mentioned the word "survival," but somehow, we all knew the test of the night.

It was cold, even with the engine running from time to time, even with the candles, even with the food breaks, even with the party talk. We were still cold.

We took turns holding Maura. I cradled her in my warm fur as best I could. Then Maggie or Tom played with her to move her arms and legs. We couldn't let her doze too long.

To keep our blood flowing, Maggie conducted an auto-aerobics course. We had to exercise once an hour, taking turns with people and body parts

so we had room to move. It was a peculiar arrangement of energy and space, and if it had been for any other reason, it would have been downright fun.

Tom must have hit his head on the ceiling light a dozen times, laughing in spite of himself. I got so excited doing fire-hydrant leg lifts that my tail kept whacking the rear window. Jumping jacks were managed without the jump, bicycle exercises were done by the front-seaters first, the back-seaters second. Waist bends were done in a kneeling position.

I skipped those. If I had a waist, I couldn't find it. Instead, I went back to doing fire-hydrant leg lifts. Some things a dog just *knows.*

Never have so many moved so much in so little room.

We played card games until Maura ate two deuces.

Tom told stories.

Maggie led songs.

Then Annie led songs.

I didn't think I could stand hearing "Happy Birthday" one more time, but Annie's heart would have been broken if anyone complained.

So we all kept cheerful. And tolerant. We had to.

We all prayed.

At six twelve, we saw the morning.

A bright orange line fringed the snow. Slowly the white world outside filled with hope.

The blizzard was over.

"Maggie, look." Tom pointed to a dark shadow less than a quarter of a mile from our car. In the cold blowing night, we did not see, could not have known, how close we were to shelter.

Hadn't the people living there seen our flare?

Perhaps they had already been asleep for the night.

"Oh, Tom!" Maggie let a tear fall for the first time. "We'll be fine now."

As the morning brightened, we could see more of the nearby house.

An old van was parked in the front yard. A summer porch swing was covered with snow. There were two outbuildings, one barn-sized and one smaller.

"Mom, there's no smoke coming from the chimney," Kathleen said. Then she added, "But maybe they ran out of firewood."

"There's a big pile of wood by that shed," Seth said, pointing to the smaller building closest to us. "Maybe they're just not up yet."

"I wouldn't have ventured out for firewood

last night either," Tom said. "People have frozen to death in their own yards doing just that."

"You can become disoriented with the blowing snow and lose your sense of direction," Maggie explained. "Should we all go up to the house at once?"

"No, Judge and I will go first. It's a longer trek than it appears," Tom said. "It just looks easy."

"I see phone lines," Seth said, "right up to the house. That's good news. The wind might have pulled them down."

"That's the first thing we'll do—call the state police and tell them our location." Tom reached clear to the back to pat my neck. "With all the drifting, I figure this is one good time to let our St. Bernard lead the way."

I was thrilled. I was not a dog of many trades, but blazing a trail on new snow was definitely one of them.

Everybody kissed us for luck.

Annie gave me three big ones.

Talk about inspiration.

Four steps from the car, I plunged nose first into a five-foot drift.

Tom laughed. "Better you than me, fella."

Well, it hadn't been the dignified start I'd hoped for, but eventually, I got my act together.

Tom had been right about there being a lot of drifts, but I followed my instincts and found the path of least resistance.

In fact, after my first humbling fall, things went almost too smoothly.

I had the uneasy feeling that the trail had already been blazed.

I couldn't actually see snowprints. The drifting would have covered them, but something about the trail made me think someone else had passed. My sniffer couldn't nail the who or what —the cold could confuse even the best noses— but I hoped that when we met the residents of the house, I could sort out the smells.

I thought of the shadow. If someone had seen us, they would have helped, wouldn't they?

An animal, perhaps, maybe even a wild animal. . . . That kind of help we didn't need.

We reached the porch. A light breeze pushed the old swing forward in a squeaky nod.

Tom and I both jumped.

"Spooked us, huh, fella?" Tom joked.

His words made my skin prickle.

Stop it, I told myself. It's daylight, we survived the blizzard, the worst is over. What's so spooky?

A stair splintered beneath my paw.

Wood rot. Or termites. The owners would

have their spring work cut out for them either way.

Our feet made the only sound. The quiet unnerved me.

My eyes were drawn to a big bay window to my right. For a strange moment I saw a reflection in the glass: brown eyes, square nose, thick fur. A cloud hid the sun and the image disappeared. Me?

Then I heard a soft thumping noise.

I looked at the window again.

Nothing.

Stupid.

Tom came up behind me.

"Hello," he called out, raising his hand to knock on the door.

He rapped gently. . . .

. . . And the front door opened . . . squeaking.

Chapter 6

"Anybody home? Hello!" Tom yelled again.

There was no answer.

We stepped inside, and the first thing we noticed was the temperature. Though it was warmer than outside, it was by no means comfortable.

"Hello?" Tom kept calling. "I don't like this."

Neither did I.

I stayed close to Tom.

The place looked like any other farmhouse. Small parlor, huge dining room, big kitchen and pantry, stairs in a large front hallway that led to second-floor bedrooms.

One dusty placemat set with silver lay on the

kitchen table. A closed jar of peanut butter was wound in cobwebs beside it. Tom picked up a moldy loaf of bread that crumbled in his hand.

I felt nauseated. Green food affected me that way.

Why would someone have left food out that long? And the door unlocked?

A wall phone was at the back door near a wood chopping block. Tom picked it up. "No dial tone," he said, shaking his head. "Of all the rural farmhouses to park in front of in a snowstorm, we pick the one with no inhabitants."

I kept trying to get my sniffer in gear. My instincts were hampered by inexperience. Okay, so there weren't inhabitants now, but there certainly had been, and there was another smell, not human. Mice, maybe?

"Still, this is better than another night in the car." Tom was reasoning out loud. "We'll tell Annie that she's going to play pioneer."

Together, we explored the entire first floor.

I stayed within six inches of Tom's left foot.

I don't know why, but I wasn't exactly crazy about a house in this state of abandonment. I fully expected a banshee to leap from one of the closets. The house just had that ghostly *feel*.

On a large bed with a handmade coverlet, a

woman's flannel nightgown lay folded. The vanity table held half-used bottles. On a chair by a window, Tom found a newspaper dated exactly three weeks ago.

Tom folded it and put it back in place, but he looked uneasy, too. Were we trespassing, or did anyone actually live here?

I pictured wild creatures lying in wait behind closed doors, and my legs began to wobble.

Silly Saint.

But the uneasy feeling didn't go away.

Spooky or not, the house was shelter. We went back to the car and got the family.

When Maggie stepped inside, she took one look around and said, "Is this house haunted or what!"

Tom shot her one of those "for heaven's sakes" looks.

"Hey, I think I'd rather stay in the car," Seth said.

"Don't be dumb. We're out of gas. Another night and we'll freeze," Kathleen said. "At least there's a fireplace and firewood in here."

"Tom, I still don't like it." Maggie was shaking her head. "We shouldn't be here. It feels funny."

"Does hawnted mean ghoses?" Annie had been thinking Maggie's words through very carefully. "Are they good ghoses or bad ghoses?"

Tom was staring at Maggie with that "It wasn't the time to open your mouth, dear" face.

"Sorry," she said. "The words just fell out."

"Never mind," said Tom. "Fact is, we're going to have to make the best of it. Surely, a state patrol will be along when the roads are clear. At least we can stay warm and dry."

"Iffen they eat peanut butter," Annie said, noticing the kitchen table, "they're prolly good ghoses."

"Did anybody check the mailbox?" Kathleen asked. "We should know who lives here, *if* someone lives here."

"I looked," Tom said. "There is no mailbox. Most of the people in these rural communities have a post office box in town and they pick up their own mail."

"Do you think they might come back while we're here?" Seth wanted to know. "I feel kinda funny staying where we're not invited."

"I can't imagine anyone not welcoming us, considering the circumstances," Maggie said. "Tom, let's look around again—thoroughly. Maybe there's farm equipment in one of the outbuildings. We might get somewhere driving a tractor that we couldn't driving a car."

"Not bad, Sherlock," Tom said. "Some of these farms have their own gas supply—we could get lucky."

"And how about food?" It was Seth. Naturally. "We could pay the owners for what we use, couldn't we?"

The snoop was on—for supplies, for a snow vehicle, for clues about the owner.

We found good news, bad news, and no news.

There wasn't any power or running water in the house, but there were plenty of dry matches and a good supply of firewood.

Tom and Maggie were surprised to find no farm equipment. Even more surprising was the discovery of a plane in the barn.

There was no tractor, no combine, not even a small mower, but a very old Cessna 150. It sat half covered with a tarp under the loft, polished and shiny on the outside, though worn and threadbare on the inside. A number of empty pesticide containers littered the dirt floor nearby, and Tom guessed that the owner had run some kind of crop-dusting operation.

"Maggie, what would you think if . . ." Tom asked, tugging the tarp away and looking at the engine.

"Don't think, dear," she answered. "Some

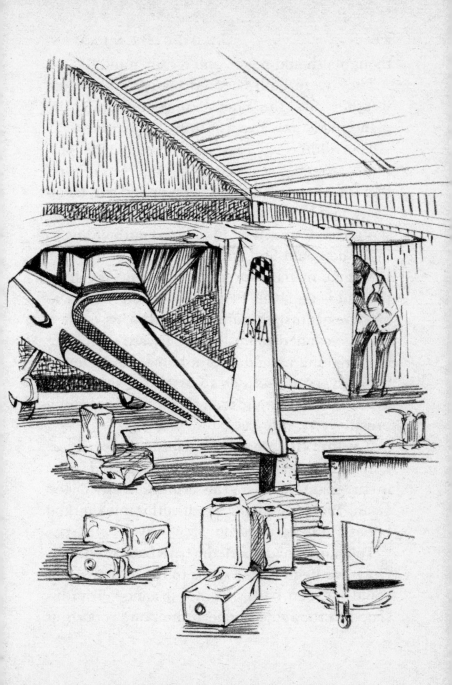

thoughts should never enter your mind."

They were both licensed pilots, but the bad weather and the uncertain condition of the plane made any attempt to fly foolhardy.

Tom didn't say anything more, but he puttered around the plane a bit. When he found that the plane's radio had been pulled out, taken apart, and left on the inside seat, he shrugged his shoulders. He went on to the next outbuilding to see if he could find anything else.

Maggie managed to assemble some revolting canned vegetables. Period. No bread, no crackers, no peanuts, just canned green beans, canned carrots, canned pinto beans—I wasn't about to eat anything named after a horse—and canned peas. Everyone refused to touch the jar of peanut butter. It sat just too close to that sickening bread.

It wasn't the breakfast our taste buds craved.

We did find lots of empty, torn bags and boxes in the pantry. Even the crumbs were licked clean. Probably some very healthy mice lurked beneath the baseboards.

Tom and I made periodic trips back to the car. Once we tied colored shirts to the antenna so it could be seen better from a distance. Tom listened to the radio to check the news reports as

regularly as he dared without completely drain-
ing the battery.

I was just as glad there had been no radio at
the house. Continued reports of closed roads and
the unpredictable storm front would not have
cheered Maggie and the kids.

For the rest of the morning, we settled in at
the farmhouse and waited for a rescue that did
not come.

By eleven o'clock, our enthusiasm began to
dampen. Heavy, dark clouds moved in to hide
the sun.

Tom came back from the latest news report
shaking his head. "We're getting another
round," he said. "Another cold front picked up
speed over the Rockies. More snow is due before
four o'clock today."

Tom and Maggie kept going over the same
ground, trying to find a solution. We were not
that far from Salem. Surely there had to be a way
to cut across the fields and get help. Or at the
very least, the snowplows would make it to us
before the next dose of snow.

Nothing in the van out front worked. From
the best Tom could determine, it hadn't been
driven for some time. He kept going back to the
barn and looking at the plane. He found the

pilot's log book and studied the notations. The name was hard to make out, but the dates were clear.

"There must have been an east-west land runway," he said out loud to himself. "But in all this snow . . ."

Maggie warmed the vegetables over the fire in the fireplace for another meal. We were too hungry not to eat something.

"I wish we hadn't used all those flares last night," Tom said.

"Tom, have you been upstairs in that little room off the small bedroom?" Maggie asked.

"No, I didn't notice that one," he said.

"Well, I couldn't get the door open, but I think it might go to the attic," Maggie said. "Farm families are usually pretty frugal—maybe they have flares or trouble lights stored up there."

I could tell by Tom's expression that he didn't think it was very likely, but it was better than sitting around.

Seth and I went with him.

Even though it was still early, the clouds had made the day look like night. Tom took the flashlight.

Something in my gut fluttered.

This house was spooky in the daytime, but the darkness made it even more so.

It took a push from all three of us to get the door opened. Tom stepped in first.

I had never before heard him scream like that.

Chapter 7

Tom fell to the floor, his hands covering his eyes. "Seth, get outa here. Bats!"

With all the flapping and thumping above us, it could have been a million of them, but when Seth moved back, shining the flashlight on the ceiling, only one flying, diving critter could be seen. It was bobbing back and forth, scaring us half to death.

When the bat landed temporarily on a lampshade, I went for it, but Seth jumped in my way. "Judge," he yelled, "we've got to keep him alive, in case he got Dad."

I only vaguely understood what he was talking

about—the bat could have bitten Tom. I hesitated, wondering just how to nail the bat with my fat paw without doing him in.

Seth didn't hesitate. With one quick swoop from behind, he bravely grabbed the bat with his bare hands!

Maggie came charging up the stairs. "What is going on?"

"Mom, get something, a box . . . or . . . or that metal wastebasket—get that!"

Maggie grabbed the wastebasket, not knowing why, and went toward her son. With one hand Seth slipped the bat toward the floor, and with the other he turned the wastebasket upside down and covered the animal.

Then he sat on it.

For a few minutes the bat flapped and fluttered. Finally, it kept still.

"Is it dead?" Maggie asked.

"No. I don't think so. Probably just asleep again," Tom said.

I will always regret what I did next. I walked toward Tom, hoping to help, and felt something sharp in my paw.

"He knocked my contact out," Tom said.

Everyone heard the crunch.

Guilt overwhelmed me.

"Well, that's that," Tom said. "You aren't the first to devastate a contact lens, Judge."

"Let's get out of here," Maggie said.

"Do you think I can get up now?" Seth asked.

"Sure, he didn't even scratch me," Tom said. "Just scared the daylight out of me. In fact, you could let the varmint go. . . ."

"Better not," Seth said softly. "He got me."

Seth held up a bloody hand.

Maggie gasped and so did I.

Tom took his handkerchief out and wrapped the wound.

"You were right about one thing. We're getting out of here." Tom led the way, bolting the attic door tightly behind us.

"Someone else can come back to examine that dumb bat," he said.

When the wound was cleaned, it looked no worse than many Seth had gotten falling off his bike. But we knew this could be a good deal more serious.

Bats carry rabies, a dreaded disease fatal to humans. The only member of the family who was routinely vaccinated against it was a certain St. Bernard.

In the moment when courage counted, Seth

had risked his life. He had not hesitated as I had.

It wasn't an act I could be proud of.

Now we *had* to get out of this snowy prison. The bat had to be tested for rabies, and Seth had to have medical attention.

Tom scooted the furniture as close to the fire Kathleen had built as he dared, so that the family could sleep warmly.

"We need special bedtime prayers tonight, kids," Maggie said, saying good night. "Pull out all the stops and ask for a miracle." She kissed four foreheads and then walked over to pat my head. "Wish I could have rustled up better food for you, fella," she said.

Her kindness made me feel worse.

I was determined to act more courageously.

I made one last patrol through the house.

I walked slowly, looking for anything I might have missed before.

It was *sooooo* dark. Only the firewood glowed. No lights inside. No lights outside.

In the kitchen I tripped over a rag rug.

It became tangled in my paw and I dragged it several feet before I shook it loose.

When I looked behind me, I saw why.

It wasn't only caught on my paw. It was hung up on the funny groove of a trapdoor.

Trapdoor? In the kitchen?

It probably led to a root cellar like the one Great-Gramps had in Metropolis. Maybe some food would be stored there. Those canned vegetables were already running low.

I took hold of the door handle with my teeth and tried to lift it, but the door slipped back.

Bump, bump.

I was ready to try again when a heard a howl.

OOOOHHHHWWWWHEEEOOO!

The heck with this discovery. If there was anything edible in there, it would wait for morning light.

I raced back to the living room into the arms of Maggie and Tom.

Chapter 8

If Maggie and Tom had heard the night cry coming from under the house, they didn't let on.

I guess they were too busy praying for a miracle.

Or else they thought it came from outside—the wind was putting up such a hoot. Had it? Or had the whole thing been my imagination? Whatever, I decided I could best serve my family by praying for a miracle, too.

Heaven knows, I couldn't sleep. The thought of something screaming in the root cellar made it tough to close my eyes. In the flicker of firelight, everything in the house looked spooky. The pictures on the wall, the lacy curtains, the trinkets on the shelves, all made curious shadows.

My heart thumped.

Nothing looked familiar, until I spotted a silver dog chain under a footstool behind the couch.

It caught my eye quite by accident when a log shifted and a rush of shining sparks flew.

It was a choke collar, like many I had worn. In fact, it appeared to be the same brand I wore once in a Canada Dog Show.

For some reason, it made me feel a bit better. I couldn't explain it, but it did. I wondered what kind of canine it had belonged to: poodle? Golden retriever? Setter? The longer I wondered, the stranger it seemed that the dog would be gone without its leash and collar. . . .

I imagined a ferocious Great Dane ghost haunting this old house—but that was utter nonsense.

Somehow, I got to sleep.

In almost no time, or so it seemed, dawn streamed through the windows.

I padded through the house before anyone else. In that clear light, much of the scariness seemed to disappear. I looked for clues to a real dog to put my ghostly fears to rest.

Thanks to my St. Bernard nose, I discovered several.

Behind a bedroom door, I found five collars.

Most were fancy, and they were big enough to fit me.

Under an old chair, I saw a grooming brush and a good-sized nipper tool for claws.

Now, I'm sure ghosts don't nip.

It had to be a privileged pet that lived here.

I felt better. I was about to further test my dog-tracking instincts when Maggie's voice rang through the house.

"It's clear outside, kids, and today we're going home. I'll just bet on it." She was checking Seth's hand when the rest of us raced to the windows.

Though the snow had swirled through the wee hours of the morning, it actually looked no worse than before. In an area in front of the barn, it looked a whole lot better. It had blown consistently in one direction, and a strip of farmyard soil peeked through.

I got excited and my tail went crazy. In a whoosh, it swept a tableful of books to the floor.

Kathleen jumped to pick them up.

I glanced down and saw several photographs that had slipped onto the floor.

As Kathleen picked them up, she shouted, "Look, Mom! Whoever lives here has a gorgeous St. Bernard!"

Seth and Annie crowded around, and so did I.

I couldn't see very well with all the bobbing heads, but it was a St. Bernard, all right. There was no date on the picture. Maybe it had been taken a long time ago.

Maggie and Tom weren't paying attention. They were having a major discussion of their own.

"I know I'm right, Tom," Maggie said. "We're talking about fifteen minutes' flying time, tops. You can't do it without your contacts, but I can."

"There's no radio, Maggie, and I don't even know if the thing will fly," Tom argued.

"That's funny. Before you had the accident with the bat, *you* were going to take it up." Maggie was smiling, but her voice was firm. "Look, Tom, the wind literally marked the grass runway. So we have to shovel twenty feet more. So what? It could be forty-eight hours before they get all these highways cleared. Do you think we can survive that long? What about Seth's injury? I don't even know what symptoms to look for, but I sure as heck figure we'd better find somebody who does. I'm sorry. I'm going whether you'll help me or not."

"Maggie, pilots, even really experienced ones, get disoriented in the snow. . . ." Tom started to say more when he looked at me and stopped suddenly. He was thinking very hard.

"The Salem airport just isn't that far," Maggie persisted.

"Okay," Tom said finally, "but you can't go alone."

He was still looking at me.

Something told me I wasn't going to like this.

Maggie seemed puzzled. "Tom, what good could the kids do?".

"Not the kids, dear," he said. "You can take Judge Benjamin."

Me? Fly? In a plane? Oh, Dumbo, where are you when I need you!

"If the worst happens and you don't make the airport, he stands a chance of getting to town for help."

"Tom, are you crazy? Judge is too heavy!" Maggie argued.

"I mean it, Maggie. You have to worry about freak gusts in a storm system like this, and icing may be a problem. Either you take the Judge or you go without my blessing," Tom said. He folded his arms in his most forceful chauvinist gesture.

Maggie was quiet. When Tom put his foot down, it was because he cared.

"It might be a good idea," she said finally. "If I stop short of Salem for any reason, he can go for help."

Wasn't anybody going to ask me what I thought?

I thought it was a lousy idea. That plane was *tiny!*

St. Bernards do not, I repeat, do not fly.

Not ever, ever, ever, ever.

I closed my eyes, trying to force out the picture of two hundred pounds of airborne dog, and in its place I imagined Trixie Lee scribbling: "EXCEPT IN A SNOWSTORM."

Chapter 9

When I thought of flying, I always pictured what it was like in First Class.

I had seen inside plenty of planes on television —leather seats, wine stewards, filet mignon, full-length movies.

That was hardly what I was facing. My first flight was to be in the Volkswagen of airplanes, the old Cessna from the barn with its patched upholstery and an inspection sticker just three weeks short of expiration. As much as I loved Maggie, I preferred a more experienced pilot, say a four-star admiral with volumes of log books.

By noon, we finished clearing the snow from the hard ground that formed the rural runway.

High noon.

I couldn't have felt lower.

Maggie and Tom went over every inch of the plane. They reassembled the radio, but it still only voiced static. Maggie hoped it would start working when we neared the Salem airport.

Seth had taken a turn listening to the weather reports and came back with the latest.

"It's clear for now, winds zero to eight, but they expect more blowing by late afternoon," he said.

"It's now or never, Tom," Maggie said, hugging her husband.

I was praying that someone would go to the barn to get me horse blinders. Or maybe a parachute. Only I didn't think Maggie intended to fly high enough for me to use one.

Instead, Annie had found two aviator scarves and two pairs of goggles, which she proudly presented to us.

Maggie started to say that we wouldn't need them, but when she saw the look on Annie's face, she put them on.

Maggie tied the white wrap around my neck and whispered, "We'll take them off as soon as we're in the air, Judge."

It occurred to me that the scarf might cover my eyes in the event that we spiraled downward. Perhaps Annie had a point.

Maggie and Tom pushed the plane to the end of the runway. "Remember, if it doesn't look like you can get your airspeed up, *don't* take off, Maggie," Tom was coaching.

"For heaven's sake, Tom, I've got as many hours as you," she answered. "It'll go. The last notation in the pilot's log says it was flown just one month ago. I'm absolutely confident."

I wished I was. Oh, how I wished I was.

Because of the need for even weight distribution in the small plane, I had to sit in the front seat.

What's more, I had to be buckled in.

That was a major hurdle. I wanted to lie flat on the seat with my face buried between my paws. But the seat belt only worked when I sat up.

I had a perfect view of the wild blue yonder. Egad.

Tom handed Maggie the sectional map with the penciled navigational markings that they had discussed. Then he walked to my side of the plane.

"Sit still, bud. You've got to sit still. This is a

little plane, and a hard sneeze affects the balance. But I need to know that Maggie's not alone," he whispered.

I thought I had been sitting still. I looked down and saw that my legs were trembling. I made a conscious effort to hold them steady.

"Hey, Mom," Seth yelled as the motor turned over, its chugging and grinding jiggling the plane. "Bring me back two Big Macs and a large order of fries!"

I tried to muster poise. I thrust my shoulders back and looked at the smiling, waving O'Rileys wishing us well—Kathleen holding Maura, Annie pulling on Kathleen's arm, Tom crossing his fingers, Seth laughing. They just stood there hopefully, watching us pick up our airspeed.

They began to blur. As the plane moved faster, everything blurred.

The plane started to really throb, and so did my heart. The speed indicator needle pushed forward.

I felt the lightness of floating the minute the wheels left the ground.

We were up, a little, then a little more.

Maggie was taking a deep breath and looking straight ahead.

I looked down.

Oh. Oh, oh.

The ground was going.

I decided it made more sense to look ahead, like Maggie.

Uh-oh.

Maggie's eyes were riveted on the telephone wires stretched across the sky at the exact altitude we seemed to be.

Maaaaggggggie!

I couldn't look. I pushed the aviator scarf over my eyes, happy for Annie's blindfold, just as we cleared the black wires.

Maggie let out a whoop. "Ah, we had at least a centimeter to spare, Judge."

I felt a hiccup coming on. A big one. It was so big, it seemed to vibrate even more than the plane.

"Hey, fella, take it easy," Maggie said. She took her hand off the controls and gave me a pat on the back.

Another hiccup exploded.

"Judge, take a deep breath. We're okay." She

patted me again. I wished she wouldn't take her hands off the controls.

"I wonder how much Dramamine a St. Bernard should take for motion sickness," she said, laughing.

Evidently the hiccups were bothering me more than Maggie.

Maggie banked the plane in a hard left, crossing over the house and climbing to a safe altitude.

I looked down once more at the O'Rileys, still watching and now really cheering. Annie was jumping up and down, and Maura had been boosted to a spot on Seth's shoulders.

Except for that patch of liveliness, the land below looked bleak with all that snow, the lonely-looking house, only a St. Bernard moving on the other side of it. . . .

St. Bernard?

Did I forget to board this plane? I had to admit my stomach felt like it was still down there.

I looked again.

Yes, there was a St. Bernard. It watched our plane for a brief moment, then disappeared into a hole at the far side of the house.

Hole? Could it have been a cellar trapdoor,

hidden by snow? Then the howl I had heard
... but why hadn't the dog come out before? And
why would a St. Bernard be there in the first
place without a master?

The plane's engine started making a peculiar
chugga-chugga noise, not at all like it had on
takeoff. I hoped it wasn't going to go into a stall.

Maggie steadied the plane, listening carefully
to the engine as it recovered its rhythm. Apparently, she was satisfied.

It seemed we were in the air a lifetime, but in
fact, it was about eight minutes when Maggie
shouted, "That's it, Judge! That's the airport!"

I answered with another lulu of a hiccup.

Maggie kept fiddling with the radio to report
our arrival, but she got only static. We could see
activity near the runways, and there were people manning the tower. Storm or not, somebody
was on the job.

I realized we'd been so busy with my fear and
Maggie's flying, we were still wearing our World
War I goodies. I did not feel particularly cute,
but it was too late to do much about it.

"We'll just have to do a flyby, Judge," Maggie
said, giving up on the radio. "I don't see any
other planes. We're going to have to go for it.

Land. Meet the ground. Oh. Oh no.

Maggie whizzed in front of the tower and waved. She must have gotten a nod from the landing tower because she throttled forward on the go-round.

"Not to worry, Judge. I can land with my eyes closed."

Dear Maggie. *Mine* are closed. Please, please, keep yours open.

The engine was making that *chugga-chugga* noise again.

I hiccuped.

The *chugga* got worse.

Maggie started whistling. I think she was nervous, too. She had never learned how to whistle, and it was a false, chirpy sound.

Hiccup.

Squeak, chirp.

I raised my head, swallowing hard to disguise the next hiccup.

The plane wasn't chugging any more. I had the distinct feeling we were losing altitude.

"This is it, Judge. We're going to land."

There were two ways to do that.

One of them rhymed with "Mash."

I held my breath and opened one eye slowly.

Chapter 10

Maggie made a perfect three-point landing.

I barely felt a bump as we touched down. She taxied as close to the tower as she dared, got out, and walked around to unbuckle me. An angry air traffic controller came racing out, shouting loudly about landing without a radio.

I stepped down.

He fainted.

I don't think he was a very tall man, but it was hard to tell when his nose and toes were both pointing skyward.

A second air traffic controller, a tall woman, was considerably more composed.

"Radio problem?" she asked.

"Yes, among other things," Maggie answered, pulling off her goggles and scarf. "My family's been stranded since the storm the night before last. We've had an emergency situation involving a bat biting my son, and we found this old plane in a barn. . . ."

"Flowers plane." The woman nodded to Maggie.

Flowers? As in rose garden?

She was telepathic, too.

"Jacob Flowers. Crop duster. Stores it at the Hoffman farm. I registered it myself." The lady indicated the sticker on the window. "He's been laid up with a broken ankle for several weeks."

"If you could tell me how to get in touch with him . . ." Maggie started to say, then moved to the more immediate problem. "But right now, I need to get help for my family, especially my son."

We were in good hands. In minutes the woman had dispatched the state police to alert the snowplow crew to get to the Ardella Hoffman residence, contacted a Southern Illinois University medical team to handle the bat emergency, and given me a big bowl of hot chocolate.

That lady knew her priorities.

Twenty-four hours later, the whole O'Riley family was sitting in the living room of our Decatur home.

"What happened to my Big Macs and fries?" Seth said. "Boy, a guy doesn't ask for much, but everybody gets hungry . . ."

Maggie threw a pillow at him.

It started a trend. The pillows really flew!

Gosh, it felt good to be home!

Seth had been lucky. The medical center personnel had picked up the bat, run tests, and pronounced the bat quite angry but not mad. No rabies.

Maggie stayed in touch with Matilda Baswanski, the air traffic controller, to tie up the loose ends of our escapade. She obtained the address of Mr. Flowers, and wrote him offering to pay him for the use of the plane. Tom settled with Mr. Flowers for the cost of the fuel and agreed to take the plane in for its inspection, since Mr. Flowers could not. He also paid Mr. Flowers for hangar storage at the Salem airport rather than making another snowy flight back to the Hoffman farm.

Matilda was not as helpful at finding Mrs. Hoffman. Her mail had been unclaimed at the post office for three weeks. The best Matilda could offer was that perhaps Ardella Hoffman had left for an unexpected trip to visit her daughter in North Carolina. She promised to look into it and get back to Maggie. She would try the small-town grapevine in Salem. It sounded a bit like Grammy's Metropolis. Someone nearly always knew what someone else was up to.

Nobody mentioned the dog. I wanted to, but I couldn't, so the St. Bernard was still a mystery.

I hoped Maggie would hear some news soon. I still couldn't figure out why that dog hadn't let us know it was there. That bothered me.

I wanted to go back to the farmhouse and play detective again, but there was no way I could have wandered as far south as Salem without worrying the O'Rileys to death. As much as I wanted to satisfy my curiosity, I knew I shouldn't venture back there alone.

Finally, I got my chance, but not in a way I expected.

Kathleen made me an honorary Girl Scout.

There was a method to her madness.

Her troop was working toward the Sign of the Arrow, a junior-ranked badge. As part of the pro-ject, her troop was to meet with another unit on a campout. Dr. Rakowski, one of the girls' fathers, offered the Scouts his log cabin on Lake Laura, just outside of Salem, and close enough to Old Salem for them to visit some historic Abraham Lincoln tourist sites. Maggie and I were "volunteered" as chaperones by Kathleen.

Maggie wasn't exactly thrilled about going camping in the middle of winter, but as long as she didn't have to sleep in a flimsy tent, she decided she could handle it.

I figured once the girls were asleep I could go back to the haunted house and see about the dog.

I had never once heard it bark. That worried me. Do ghosts bark? What was I thinking?

The trip to the lake was one giant choral fest —four cars and one camper full of giggling, crooning girls. The few times the girls in our car took a break between songs like "Jacob's Ladder" and "Ninety-nine Bottles of Beer on the Wall," they told riddles. And elephant jokes. Now and then, I suppose to entertain me, they told stories about their pets.

No one had an elephant.

Enough snow remained from the early season's blizzard to cover the ground, but the sky was blue and clear, indicating good weather.

I was glad. One blizzard was enough for my taste.

Dr. Rakowski's cabin was set on lovely rolling hills. Trees grew sparsely here and there.

From the farthest hill on the doctor's property, I could see several farms. Nearest, and I could hardly believe my good fortune, was Mrs. Hoffman's house. It stood gray and sad, more so than I had remembered.

I could see no sign of life. I couldn't see much of anything, actually. When the girls got ready to go to sleep . . . I would . . ."

"Judge Benjamin! Come!" Maggie called, interrupting my plans.

I went at a gallop.

"We've assigned you to bathroom duty," she said, smiling.

Bathroom duty?

It didn't take long to figure out that what I had to do would be a full-time job. One thing missing in Dr. Rakowski's marvelous prairie cabin was indoor plumbing.

When Kathleen first arrived, she reacted as if a bomb had been dropped.

"I don't believe it! He has real leather chairs, priceless Oriental rugs, quarry stone in the fireplace, and no toilet?"

"It's primitive but practical," Maggie had explained. "The biggest problem with vacation houses is that their pipes burst in the cold winters when they are vacant. Dr. Rakowski has a pump connected to the kitchen sink that draws from the well and can be disconnected anytime. But bathroom plumbing, that's a bit more complicated."

"Mom, did you see that *thing!* It's gross. I mean really *gross!* There's no light, and it will be full of bugs and ishies and it smells awful."

"There won't be bugs when it's this cold," Maggie said. "Just take some deodorant spray and a flashlight. You'll live."

I had to admire Maggie's stoic attitude. I knew the thought of an outdoor john made her just about as enthusiastic as Kathleen, but she was hiding her misery well.

Amazing how motherhood makes one rise above things.

I had been right about my full-time job.

By bedtime, I knew every girl—forty-one in all—by her first name, because each had made at least three trips.

Tiffany Lloyd had made seven.

I suspected she just liked walking in the snow with me, but I didn't mind. I heard Alice Grew say Tiffany's goldfish had died the week before, and I was a new practice pet.

I wondered how her mother would adjust to a two-hundred-pound eating hulk after having a small swimming creature in a bowl. Tiffany seemed to think it was perfectly natural.

By midnight, the girls had cooked hot dogs and sloppy joes, warmed fried pies, sung Christmas carols—they had sung everything else they knew on the way down—exchanged troop stories, played rhythm till their thighs stung from slapping, roasted marshmallows, drank hot chocolate, and finally crawled into their sleeping bags to sleep on the floor of the cabin's great room near the crackling fire.

Maggie and the other drivers and chaperones finished cleaning what was left of the mess. They lugged the trash bags away from the cabin toward the cars. No one really expected wild animals to be attracted by the food smells, but better to be safe than sorry.

I had planned to make my way to the Hoffman house while everyone slept, but the seven sloppy joes, five hot dogs, and assorted carbohydrates I had devoured made me sleepy.

Morning would be soon enough.

I had barely nodded off when I heard Kathleen whisper, "It's Tiffany again, Judge. Me too."

Duty had its moments of glory, but this wasn't one.

After sitting by that warm fire, the walk was supercold and longer than my tired bones wanted to travel.

I stood outside the "thing" waiting for Tiffany and Kathleen, my eyelids drooping.

I made myself study the landscape and count trees backward. There weren't that many, so I started to add cars and garbage cans.

One can jumped.

Jumped?

I smelled trouble.

I didn't know whether to investigate or stay close to the girls. I remembered my hesitation with the bat and pressed forward.

A large, furry shadow had grabbed one of the bags of garbage, shaking it hard till the contents popped the plastic.

Splat. Goop spewed everywhere.

And that was only the first bag.

Oh, pooh.

I had hoped for a nice quiet night. But I wouldn't be doing my duty if I didn't chase whatever it was away.

Not feeling particularly brave, which is my

normal condition, I chose my most passive weapon, noise.

I woofed, a good, loud, long St. Bernard woof.

I didn't count on it echoing, but back across the snow it came, *woof, woof.*

Double woofies?

That was no echo. The intruder spoke my language.

I barked again. Garbage or not, the animal was trespassing.

WOOOOOOF!

Kathleen and Tiffany came out of the latrine.

"Judge Benjamin! You'll wake everybody up!" Kathleen scolded.

Tiffany came running up to me, gripping her parka with one hand and holding her flapping bathrobe at the ankles with the other.

It couldn't be done. Not by a master magician.

Tiffany tumbled headfirst into the snow, rolling into Kathleen's heels.

Kathleen's hands hit the snow a split second before her face did.

Ooooch!

Meanwhile, the woof echo got louder.

Only this time it wasn't just *woof.* It was *snarl, growl, woof, snarl.*

Now, I am not a violent dog. But as the snarl

came closer, I figured this character wasn't about to sign a treaty. I had to deal with this enemy somehow.

Kathleen and Tiffany recovered from the fall and raced toward the cabin.

It was up to me.

I walked as close as I dared and looked past the snarl, past the growl. I saw a thin, tired St. Bernard. Her black mask could once have been a reflection of my own.

She wore a beautiful leather collar.

This was no ghost. This was a dog half starved and fighting for her food. Those eyes were kind. Only the bark was angry.

Slowly, steadily, I walked up and touched my paw to her shoulder. For a brief moment her jaw relaxed.

Suddenly there was an explosion of humans. Maggie, the leaders and chaperones, and forty-one girls came storming out the cabin door, screaming, "Charge!"

It had been a quickly planned, masterfully executed war ploy.

The adults carried brooms and shovels, while Mrs. Dubs waved a Teflon spatula as if it were a deadly bayonet. The girls dug in by the bushes near the porch and the snowballs flew.

"See the foam on its mouth?" Tiffany yelled. "It's mad, it is!"

Foam? You mean the marshmallow goo from the garbage?

No one got close enough to check. They just kept attacking.

Their intentions were honorable. Their aim was terrible.

Georgette Bearint hit the brooms and me four times.

Maggie got sacked by a misthrow from Callie Gibbons.

But the strategy worked. The dog ran away. Thin as she was, her retreat was dignified and speedy.

I wished I could have had more time with her. Something told me there were two sides to her story, and we had only seen one.

Chapter 11

We left very early the next morning.

Maggie never let me out of her sight, though I desperately wanted to find the other St. Bernard.

I had a job to do, so I stayed.

Mrs. Dubs called the local authorities about the dog, but they said it was out of their jurisdiction. Unless the dog appeared within the city limits, they could do nothing about it.

Thank goodness.

I still believed there was a lot to learn about that dog. If only Maggie had word from Matilda about Mrs. Hoffman's daughter . . . but there was no message waiting for us when we got home.

We did find mail, though, lots of it. The big family Thanksgiving dinner was scheduled to take place at our house in Decatur, and from the news in our box, we could expect a full house. A very full house. Everyone in our family was automatically welcome, no matter how far away they lived.

The week before Thanksgiving, Maggie and the kids scoured every nook and cranny in the house. Tom and Seth cleaned the inside pool, too, laying in enough chemical supplies to keep the water fresh for lots of swimming. The freezer nearly popped its hinges with cooked meals that Maggie froze ahead. The last thing she did on Wednesday before the overnight guests started ringing the doorbell was to put the thirty-pound turkey in a Styrofoam cooler to thaw slowly.

Within an hour after people started arriving, the house was wall-to-wall relatives and their related beasts.

The driveway looked like a used-car parking lot. There were cars and campers everywhere. Uncle Joe did the unthinkable, hooking a U-Haul to his prize Porsche to handle the overflow of toys, luggage, and stuff. Uncle Joe seldom could get away for vacations, so when he did take one, he made the most of it and stopped to see every relative along the way. He and his family had visited a great aunt in Kentucky already, and on the trip back toward Nashville, they planned to stop in Joe's hometown, Salem, where his folks still lived.

Small-towners are so good at keeping tabs on people, even after they move away, that I wondered if Maggie would ask him about Mrs. Hoffman. There was a chance his mother might shed some light on her disappearance, even if Uncle Joe didn't know anything.

The day was too hectic to ask.

There was just so much laughing, cooking, eating, and playing, who could think about anything but family?

Aunt Martha and Uncle Dick brought their son and daughter and Ginger, a small, quiet, older dog they had recently adopted. Ginger cased the place for the perfect spot to spend the day and chose the padded chair on the deck by the pool. She didn't budge. Aunt Martha served Ginger's meals on a tray.

Uncle Joe's U-Haul held an additional surprise, a *big* surprise. Besides dirt bikes and assorted suitcases, Aunt Ellen had packed her cats.

Maggie took a very deep breath and settled

the kitty litter box in the laundry room. Then she fixed a *large* batch of cranberry daiquiris for happy hour.

I was introduced to the felines immediately.

Aunt Ellen told me I would just love them.

For the sake of peace, I tried.

The mother cat was named Rover. She was plump and white with pink ears and rhinestones around her neck. She primped constantly.

Two of the kittens, Clara and Harold, looked like carbon copies of their mother. Harold walked into the dining room mirror—four times. Dumb! Clara spent a half-hour watching an ant carry a crumb across the patio and then ate the ant to get the crumb. The third kitten, the only one that was solid black, was named Snowball.

The logic of their names escaped me. Mark, Uncle Joe and Aunt Ellen's youngest, tried to explain that if one of the white ones had been called Snowball, it would have been too confusing.

This wasn't?

Maggie had a huge pot of potato soup simmering on the stove, and Clara sat underneath to catch drips before they hit the floor.

She wasn't just fast, she was a real chow hound —or should I say chow cat?

Anyway, in Clara's eagerness to grab the soup, she usually wound up under someone's foot.

Mostly Maggie's.

After seeing Maggie trip for the fourth time, Tom announced that it was time to go swimming.

"Let's put the cats in the laundry room," he said tactfully. "You know how cats hate getting wet."

Maggie and I both relaxed.

Diplomacy is a nice thing to witness.

Ginger and I sat by the pool and watched everyone swim. Most of the time, we got regularly doused. Uncle Joe's dives made everyone laugh. He would say he was going to do a "steak knife" and "robin" and "hamburger twelve." Then he would belly-flop exactly the same way every time.

The kids played water tag, and the wives trounced the husbands in a game of volleyball.

It was so much fun, nobody left the water, even for a towel. The least busy place was next to the extra clothes drier by the pool that Maggie used to keep the pool towels fresh. So when I got tired of the noise, I lay down there for a breather.

In spite of the giggles and shouts from the

pool, I heard a most peculiar thumping noise in my corner. At first I thought there was a problem with the pool equipment located in the laundry room below.

But then I realized that motors don't meow.

Both the drier in the laundry room below and the drier by the pool had the same vent.

I heard a distinct rubbing noise behind the drier door.

It defied logic, but I suspected one of the kittens had made the trip upstairs via the vent. It was nearly straight up and slippery, and it had to be a pretty dumb feline to even consider. . . . Then I had a gut feeling about just which not-so-brilliant-kitten might try such nonsense.

Sure enough, the door finally popped open.

There sat Harold.

Now, most cats are simply not crazy about water. They have a kind of self-employed mouth-to-paw cleaning service. But Harold did have a thing about his own reflection.

When he saw the water, he couldn't resist taking a peek at himself.

He bent over the corner of the pool, watching the waves distort his image.

Hmmm.

Nobody noticed him except me. Who would be looking for a cat by the pool?

He was not happy about the wavy distortions. So he reached a paw out to swat one away.

Splash. In he went.

I was there before he sank, grabbing him in my big mouth and hauling him out. He was sputtering water.

Still nobody noticed.

Harold had swallowed a lot of pool. I figured somebody should have a look at him.

There was only one member of the family who was not swimming.

Ginger.

I deposited Harold neatly in her lap and waited for the howl.

She didn't let me down. That whiny bark could have broken glass.

The pool was instantly evacuated.

Chapter 12

Harold's mistake was nothing compared to Clara's.

At four A.M., the morning of Thanksgiving, Maggie yawned her way to the kitchen to stuff the turkey.

When Maggie opened the Styrofoam cooler to take out the plump bird, she found a mutilated carcass instead. By no stretch of the imagination could what remained of the turkey be considered edible. A very overstuffed animal *was* in the room, but it was no bird. It was Clara, moaning under the table.

There was no way to buy and cook another turkey before dinner that afternoon. So the table

was set with mashed potatoes, assorted vegetables, salads, Jell-O, sweet potatoes, pumpkin pie,
plum pudding, and scrambled eggs.

Tom made a great pretense of carving the
scrambled eggs.

No turkey, no gravy, no dressing, but it was
great. The only one that didn't enjoy the meal
was Clara. I had a feeling she wasn't going to eat
again for several days.

I hated to see everyone leave on Friday,
Aunt Ellen and Uncle Joe were the last to go.

Uncle Joe stood on the porch talking while
Aunt Ellen rounded up the kids and cats.

"Best turkey I ever ate," Uncle Joe was saying.
"You can always tell when the fowl is fresh."

Maggie just shook her head.

"And so *big*," Uncle Joe exaggerated. "Why, it
was forty pounds if it was an ounce." With that
he spread his arms in a huge circle and knocked
the mailbox off its hinges.

"Oops, sorry," he said, picking up the metal
container. An envelope that must have been
stuck to the bottom dropped to the porch. Uncle
Joe bent to pick it up. "You missed one."

"Oh, great," Maggie said, looking at the postmark. "I've been waiting for this."

Uncle Joe was looking at the postmark, too.

"Salem?" I didn't know you had friends there."

Maggie explained briefly about the search for Ardella Hoffman. ". . . So we've been trying to contact her daughter. . . ."

"You mean Carol?" Uncle Joe asked. "Married a Clint. They're in some kind of boutique business. She's out of the country half the time on buying trips. Big job! You're lucky you heard from her this soon."

"Well, Matilda from the airport must have found her and given her our address. But I'm afraid Carol couldn't tell us what we need to know. She had no idea her mom wasn't at home in Salem." Maggie finished reading the letter, frowning.

Kathleen came out on the porch, lugging Rover. "Did you know Mrs. Hoffman when you were living in Salem, Uncle Joe?"

"Everybody knew Mrs. Hoffman. If you were a friend of Carol's, you could ride their horses anytime," he said. "Why didn't you mention that was the house where you had your crazy camping trip?"

Maggie was rereading the letter and didn't answer.

"We didn't see any horses," Seth said, dragging a dirt bike toward the U-Haul.

"Not likely anymore," said Uncle Joe. "When Mr. Hoffman died, Ardella got rid of the animals."

"Not all of them," Aunt Ellen added, walking by with a suitcase and two grocery bags of dirty clothes. "Remember that gorgeous St. Bernard Carol brought one Christmas? That was Mrs. Hoffman's pride and joy."

I thought of the thin, haggard dog I had seen. Pride and joy? Something was very wrong.

Mark fell out of the crab apple tree, and Aunt Ellen went to investigate.

Tom rubbed his chin thoughtfully. "Joe, how far out of your way would it be to drive by the Hoffman place and see if Ardella made it back from wherever she went?"

"Happy to," Uncle Joe said. "We run out of things to do when we visit my folks anyway. The boys will like a chance to spread their wings. I'll just turn them loose with their bikes on all that acreage."

Jack came whooshing past on the second dirt bike. He rode it straight into the trailer.

I don't know exactly what came over me. I kept thinking of that St. Bernard I had seen, Mrs. Hoffman's "pride and joy." I had to find that dog. No master or mistress would have abandoned a loved animal for nearly a month. And a dog that had been pampered for all of its life would not be able to manage without its owner's love.

She would starve.

I had to do it. My only chance was during the confusion of the usual good-bye kissing and hugging. Maybe no one would notice me stow away.

Just after Snowball was put into the U-Haul and Harold ran out of it and into the yard, I saw my opening. I hoped no one would see me go.

I crawled into the back of the trailer and lay down behind the dirt bikes. Rover and Clara gave me a funny look but began cleaning their paws.

Mark threw Harold into the U-Hall without so much as a glance in my direction.

Uncle Joe fired the Porsche engine like a jet.

It didn't bother me a bit.

After flying in a little Cessna, hitchhiking was going to be easy as pie.

Chapter 13

Harold sat on my tongue most of the way.

November or not, the trailer was stuffy and hot.

Uncle Joe had lined the bottom with wool army blankets to keep the cold out. It kept everything else out, too. Like air. For breathing.

So I panted. The instant my tongue left my mouth, Harold waltzed over and parked his bottom on it.

I faked a sneeze to get rid of him, but he came back.

Finally, I stood and boosted myself up against one of the dirt bikes. I pushed open the flap on top of the trailer to get some fresh air.

I could roughly fill one nostril, but by turning my head at a certain angle, I could also see outside with one eye.

It improved the trip immeasurably.

I kept going over what I would do once I got to Salem. If Uncle Joe stopped at his parents' home first, maybe I could sneak out of the trailer and try to find the Hoffman house myself. If Uncle Joe discovered me, he wasn't going to be too happy about my hitching a ride. He would probably feel responsible for getting me back to Decatur.

I began to feel guilty.

If only I had planned things first, then acted.

But the St. Bernard that I had seen on the Scout trip was hungry and alone, and I wanted to help. Somehow I intended to get her back to Decatur, where the O'Rileys could feed her until her mistress returned. Maggie would have wanted me to. Annie would have wanted me to. Kathleen would have insisted, if she had known, that we take care of an abandoned dog. Maura? Tom? Well, I couldn't be sure of Tom, but I figured Maura would convince him with a few happy gurgles.

When we got to Salem, Uncle Joe didn't drive to his parents' house first. Instead he drove to

Mrs. Hoffman's house since it was right on the highway.

There was a crowd of people in the driveway.

I recognized the flashing blue lights of the state police cars and the bright red one glowing on top of the car that read County Sheriff.

Uncle Joe rolled down the window of his Porsche and waved to the sheriff like it was old home week. "Hey, Allen, what's going on?"

Was there anybody Uncle Joe didn't know?

I had to strain to hear. The sheriff was saying things like "boarding up" and "property to be auctioned" and "not the first time Ardella disappeared, but the longest." If Mrs. Hoffman's St. Bernard had been able to manage before, she certainly couldn't now. Her home was being sold out from under her.

And where was the dog?

If it had been me, seeing a sheriff, police, and guns in my driveway, I probably would have taken off. For where? Where would she have gone? She couldn't have traveled far. The sheriff said everyone had arrived only minutes before Uncle Joe.

I had to act fast.

I needed a diversion.

I looked at Harold and decided he was dumb

enough to help. What's more, he owed me something after parking on my tongue for half the
trip and being saved from a watery grave in the
Decatur pool.

I waited until the sheriff was walking away.
Then I pushed Harold through the flap and over
the edge of the U-Haul.

Harold landed on the sheriff's shoulder, then
somersaulted to the ground and raced away.

Everybody started chasing him.

I pushed open the trailer door and made my
exit, diving behind a huge old hickory tree at the
end of the yard.

I paused for a breather, looked up, and saw a
dark furry blur running away.

It didn't take much to overtake her. Her speed
dwindled with each step. She was even thinner
than I remembered, but when I caught up with
her, she didn't growl. She simply stopped, sat
down, and faced me.

Finally, I was going to learn the other side of
the story.

Chapter 14

A narrow brass nameplate hung from her collar.
It read "Agatha Bliss Hoffman" in perfect script.
The I.D. collar sagged loosely from her neck,
much too loosely. She was so thin.

She sat very still studying me.

I wanted to be her friend. I barked softly.

Her eyes showed alarm instantly as she
glanced over my shoulder to the police cars be-
yond.

Dodo. Why did I always do the dumb thing?

Agatha must have sensed my discomfort. This
time it was she who put her paw to my shoulder.
I followed her to the cover of a mulberry brush.

We sat there catching our breath, our eyes glued to the noisy activity of the farmhouse.

Harold had been corralled. The police were nailing plywood on the windows, and the sheriff was posting signs on the porch.

Agatha winced every time another piece of glass was covered, but she kept watching.

When they finished on the side nearest us, Agatha sat up suddenly, her back arching and her ears rising.

She looked at me, then back at the house.

Uncle Joe and the sheriff were walking toward us!

Had they seen me after all?

We held our breath. The sun glinted on the silver revolver in the sheriff's holster, and suddenly I knew how a wild dog must feel in the presence of humans.

Twenty feet from where we hid, they stopped.

I gulped and instantly regretted it.

I sounded like a toilet plunger.

Apparently, they didn't hear me.

Thank goodness.

Uncle Joe offered a cigarette to the sheriff, but he refused it. "Gave those up four years ago," he said.

"But I know Carol Hoffman can afford the taxes," Uncle Joe was saying.

"Sure," the sheriff answered, "but what's the point? Mrs. Hoffman's had spells before, each one worse than the last. If she can be found this time, she's going to have to be helped. Hanging on to this farmhouse isn't what she needs. When, and if, we find her, she'll have to go to Carol's."

"I've heard of Alzheimer's disease, but I never really knew how tragic . . ." Uncle Joe looked back at the lonely house.

"So many diseases with so many pills to cure them, but not this one." The sheriff shook his head. "In the beginning it was mild. She had some confusion with numbers and dates, and she couldn't remember where she put things. Then Ardella began mixing up time and place. She'd forget to eat, forget to wash. Her mind just couldn't figure things out. One day we found her at the abandoned schoolhouse."

Uncle Joe sat down on the ground, and the sheriff joined him. The sheriff kept talking. "She was just sitting in one of those little desks with her arms folded like the perfect student. We never would have known she was there if it hadn't been for that dog, barking and making a fuss outside."

"The dog? You mean her St. Bernard? What happened to the dog?"

"Well, that's another funny thing," the sheriff said. "For a while, the dog followed her and kind of watched over Ardella. When folks saw it making a commotion, they figured Ardella needed help and somebody saw that she got home okay. But after that day at the schoolhouse, Ardella got very agitated, kept talking about schools being no place for dogs—I really don't know."

I could feel a shudder go through Agatha. The memory had to be painful. Something very powerful had kept her from staying with Ardella that last time she took off.

"You mean Ardella didn't even remember that the dog was hers?" Joe looked shocked.

"Nobody knows what she thought. Old Man Flowers would come out and leave food and water for the Saint. Awhile back, he and Carol had talked about selling the dog to a kennel in Wisconsin. . . ."

So of course Agatha had hidden. She had tried to stay with her mistress to help for as long as she could.

"Then he got laid up. We don't know." The sheriff scratched his chin and was quiet.

"Such a beautiful animal. If anyone knew the situation—"

The sheriff interrupted, "That's what I figured. Chances are she was stolen and sold."

I watched Agatha carefully. It had suited her that everyone believed she was gone. She needed to be there in case Ardella came back.

Now the sheriff was preparing to auction the property and send Ardella to her daughter.

The last of her home and hope were gone.

Agatha looked at me, and I understood.

I had enough home for both of us. I would get her back to Decatur, somehow.

Aunt Ellen came walking up, holding Harold under her arm. "Kids are getting restless, Joe," she said.

"Sure, hon. I'm coming," Uncle Joe said.

He and the sheriff got up. Harold, in his typical stupid reaction to anything, jumped out of Ellen's arms and ran away from the sheriff . . .

. . . toward our mulberry bush.

He ran within two feet, stopped, and stared.

My heart was racing. Was this idiot cat going to blow our cover?

Aunt Ellen was still standing in the same place, yelling, "Harold, so help me, if you don't come back right now, we're leaving you."

He didn't. They turned, determinedly, and walked back toward the car.

Cats aren't the kind of animal to come on command, but Harold was so dumb, he didn't seem to know that. After fifty seconds of indecision, he turned around and headed after Joe and Ellen, his tail dragging between his short, fat legs.

Whew!

Agatha sighed.

I sighed.

We watched the people get in their cars and leave. Once again the farmhouse was lonely and quiet. I looked at Agatha.

Her face said, "What next?"

My heart was saying the same thing.

I knew we couldn't walk back to Decatur. And she needed food.

I said a silent prayer. A picture of Trixie Lee and her pan of milk at Sandoval popped into my head.

I remembered the Sandoval truck stop and the nice people there. If we could find another truck stop, we might have the same good luck and find food. What's more, some of those trucks would be heading toward Decatur. Maybe we could hitch a ride. It might work.

I stood up and started to lead the way, but Agatha didn't follow me. She had been having some thoughts of her own. She was walking toward the house. When I barked, she turned back to me. Her expression spoke volumes. She wanted one last look.

I followed her.

She went directly to the side of the house where I had first seen her. A pile of mulberry branches hid the one opening the police had missed, a cellar coal chute. She pulled the branches aside.

It hardly seemed big enough for my two hundred pounds, but I squeezed through.

In the dark room, I saw how Agatha had had to live. Broken mason jars were everywhere. She had had to pick through the glass to eat the food. When the shelves were empty, she had resorted to the ways of a wild dog. . . . I turned my head away from those remains.

Agatha stood on a wooden crate and pushed her nose and shoulders to open the trapdoor.

It gave way. It was the trapdoor to the kitchen that I had found.

We climbed into the house.

There was very little light with the windows boarded, but I could see things come to life that I hadn't even noticed when we were there in the snowstorm. A blanket with Agatha's name was pushed under the bed, and stacks of photos were piled in open boxes under other beds. There were pictures of a fine Saint Bernard puppy growing into a beautiful dog. A Christmas stocking was folded carefully in the corner of a window seat. It had faded green-and-red stripes, and sequins were sewn onto the stretchy fabric. Glued to the toe of the stocking, I saw a laminated picture of a laughing Ardella holding a fluffy St. Bernard pup. It's head peeked out of the top of the stocking. . . . It was the only time Agatha whimpered.

When she had composed herself, she picked up the stocking and led the way out.

We went back through the trapdoor, pulling the rope to close it as she must have done many times in her hiding. We climbed through the cellar chute and kept going.

We didn't look back. She had decided to trust me, and I had to believe in myself.

We walked along Route 51 until we found what I had prayed for.

The building at the side of the road could have doubled for the one in Sandoval. It had a flat-roofed diner, a gas station to the right, and a large gravel driveway that could handle lots of truck traffic.

What's more, the people were just as delightful.

The meal of the day must have been open-faced roast beef sandwiches with mashed potatoes and gravy. The leftovers people gave us were pretty soggy, but Agatha thought they were scrumptious. I couldn't wait to see her enjoy Maggie's cooking.

We were given a variety of odds and ends, too. We shared half a hot dog, a lot of bread crusts, and a corner of chocolate cake.

When we had our fill, I looked for a truck headed for Decatur. Within an hour, a small open-ended van with TOM'S PRODUCE IN DECA-TUR written on the side pulled up. It was nearly filled with crates of oranges and grapefruits, but Agatha and I jumped in the back while the driver was in the diner. We squeezed ourselves next to the spare tire, where we hoped we wouldn't be noticed.

I had to make one quick trip back to the cor-

ner of the truck stop when Agatha remembered
that she'd left her stocking there.

When I returned with her treasure, she made
me feel like a hero for having bothered.

Pleasing her was so easy.

In a few minutes, the truck driver returned
and we started moving north. For one bumpy
hour, we rode along, counting the stars as they
came out, studying the moon, dreaming dreams.

I felt I had always known Agatha Bliss. And I
believed that from now on, I would always want
to.

Our peaceful ride was interrupted by a loud
bang and a hard swerve to the shoulder of the
road.

Darn. A flat tire. And we still had a long way
to go.

Agatha and I jumped out before the driver
came around to get the spare.

I saw the shadow of a burly, bearded man mut-
tering angrily.

It was unlikely we'd form a permanent friend-
ship.

Agatha took one quick glance at him, at me,
and then we bounded down into the ditch by the
side of the road.

I was feeling a bit hopeless. We could wait till the tire was changed, or move up the road and try to hitch again. . . . Then what looked like a rocket shot down the highway. Its tires squealed, it turned around, and it rocketed back.

I would have recognized Uncle Joe's Porsche anywhere!

He got out to help the trucker. "Trouble?"

The man nodded.

Uncle Joe rolled up his sleeves and went to work.

"Did you stop at the truck stop a ways back?" Uncle Joe asked.

The man nodded again. Big talker, that one.

"I'm looking for a couple of hitchhikers." Joe was studying the back of the truck. He'd be looking toward the ditch next. I began to feel trapped. "St. Bernards, two of 'em. A waitress noticed them hanging around. She thought she saw 'em get in your truck."

This time the man grunted.

I wasn't sure what that meant. Neither was Uncle Joe.

"Sure wish I could find them. They've got a lot of folks worried," Joe said.

Suddenly I realized what a terrible scare I must have given the O'Rileys.

I stepped out into the road and barked.

Agatha hesitated only a minute, then stood right behind me.

"I knew it!" Uncle Joe yelled. "I've been on the phone speculating with Maggie, and I just knew it! C'mon, you two. I'm taking you home to Decatur."

The truck driver nodded in our direction, finished the last lug, and got up.

"Hope they didn't eat my fruit." It was the only thing he had to say.

Chapter 15

Four of us made the speedy trip north to Decatur. Uncle Joe, Agatha, Harold, who rode on the
dash staring at my mouth in search of a tongue,
and me. We were so crowded that Joe didn't
light even one cigarette and that made him
drive much faster. We threatened to crack the
sound barrier as we whizzed along. I almost
wished a policeman would pull us over just so I
could see the look on his face. It was a good thing
Joe had disconnected the U-Haul before he went
looking for me, or it would have self-discon-
nected.

When we pulled into the O'Riley driveway,

Uncle Joe honked a loud greeting. The whole family came racing out onto the porch.

"He's home! Judge is home!" Kathleen yelled.

I was hugged nearly to suffocation. Maura couldn't get close enough to grab hold of my fur, so she went over to Agatha. She looked at the funny stocking Agatha held in her mouth, pulled it out, draped it on her ears, and then gave her a giant welcome hug.

I could see Agatha's tension melt. Now the stocking held a new memory.

Annie marched up to the top step of the porch where everyone could see her, planted her fists on her hips, and in her best Mommy voice shouted, "Judge Bejmin! Where haf you bin?"

"Filling my U-Haul and my Porsche with dog hairs, for one thing!" Uncle Joe told everyone. "When I called Maggie to tell her about Mrs. Hoffman and she explained that the Judge was missing—well, it didn't take a super sleuth to put the pieces together," Uncle Joe added.

Maggie was petting Agatha. "Get a big bowl of milk, Seth, and see if you can find some leftover roast, Kathleen. We had no idea we'd lose one Saint and find two!"

"I didn't know I'd get that lucky either, Maggie," Joe said. "I could have sworn I saw a St.

Bernard when we first pulled up at the Hoff-
mans. And then the hair in the trailer that
couldn't have been from our cats . . . ."

"What made you go to that truck stop to in-
quire?" Kathleen asked, putting a plate of leftovers in front of Agatha.

"Are you kidding? That's the highway grapevine. You don't grow up in a small town and not
know that," Joe explained.

"I was able to get in touch with Carol, Joe. You
were right. She would love it if we would take
care of Agatha," Maggie said. "And I don't know
quite how to thank you for making another trip
back."

"Forget it," Uncle Joe said. " 'Course, it
wouldn't hurt if you could scrounge up a piece
of that lemon meringue pie I had to leave earlier."

We all marched into the kitchen to raid the
refrigerator.

Annie steered Agatha by her ear, but she
didn't seem to mind a bit.

"Carol isn't going to change her mind and
want Agatha later, is she?" Seth was feeding
Doritos to Agatha. She wouldn't stay thin long.
"And if they find Mrs. Hoffman . . . ."

"I sincerely hope they do, but no, she can no

longer be responsible for her pet," Maggie said.

"I'll be 'sponsible for Agafa," Annie said.

Tom got up and patted Agatha. "It's settled, then. The O'Rileys are a two–St. Bernard family."

"Just two? Seth laughed. "What if they have puppies?"

"Puppies? *Puppies!*" Annie screamed.

Somehow this conversation was moving a bit fast for me.

Uncle Joe got up to leave. "On that happy note, I . . ."

Happy note?

We walked him to the car. There was a scramble to find Harold who was standing on the bathroom sink, studying himself in the mirror. Kathleen handed him to Uncle Joe through the car window.

Once more the rocket took off.

In the pause as we watched him drive away, Annie returned to her train of thought. "Yup, puppies, St. Bernard puppies. Wow."

"Hold it. This house is only so big," Maggie said.

"We can have forty." Annie only heard what she wanted to hear. "But then they hab to git married."

I didn't really like the way Annie phrased that, but I had to admit that the idea was sort of appealing.

Agatha didn't flinch. In fact, I detected the slightest happy twinkle each time the word "puppy" was spoken.

We filed back into the house. Kathleen had gotten a broom and dustpan to sweep up the Dorito mess. "Annie, dogs don't get married."

"But they hab puppies, you said so. And Mommy says—"Annie would have gone on, but Kathleen interrupted her.

"Okay, okay! I heard that part of the story. But it's just a figure of speech. I mean, we don't need a priest or a justice of the peace or something like that for dogs." Kathleen shook her head. Explaining anything to Annie required considerable persistence and patience.

Maggie pulled her head out of the refrigerator, two hot dogs in hand. Agatha and I each got one. "Nice thought, though, dearie," she said, smiling at Annie. "A little ceremony is good for the soul."

"Mommy, why not?" Annie wasn't letting up.

Agatha raised an ear, and I could feel a blush coming on.

"Well . . ." Maggie began assembling a heap of

goodies for a final snack. "I suppose we could have a pretend wedding."

Wedding? *Wedding?*

"No, it can't be pretend," Annie said firmly. "It's got to be real."

The fine line between real and pretend was confusing, to say the least. I know *I* was confused.

Seth was eating lunch meat faster than Maggie could put it on a plate. "I'll be the priest, Annie. I've heard the words often enough while serving Mass as an altar boy. 'For better or worse, and even if you're sick and poor, never to perish in measles . . .' "

Kathleen shook her head and sighed.

She wasn't the only one.

All the talk about being sick and perishing and measles . . .

"No, it's gotta be a real priest. Thas the right way," Annie insisted.

"Now, Annie, I could be persuaded to go along with this little ceremony, but you have to make some compromises," Maggie said.

"We can hab as many mices as you want." Annie was missing the point, but somewhere between Cinderella and reality, Annie was planning a wedding.

"No, dear, I mean, you will have to settle for only family members taking part," Maggie explained more simply.

"No priest? No altar? But Mommy!" Annie was about to burst into tears.

"What's this priest stuff?" Tom chimed in. "The captain of a ship can perform a wedding, and I'm the captain around here."

Maggie turned to look at Tom. "That's odd. I thought we were co-captains." She raised one eyebrow.

So did Agatha.

The female mind is not something to mess around with. We males have to communicate verrrrry carefully.

"Of course. That's exactly what I meant," Tom said, backstepping, then conveniently changing the subject. "The ketchup just overflowed the dish."

"Okay. You cin both be priests," Annie said.

Yup. Another feminist in the family and barely three years old.

"And we need an altar. No, we need a ship." Annie was talking so much that no one was listening anymore.

Ship?

"And we'll hab it in the pool. . . ."

Someone heard that. Kathleen. "What? Annie, for heaven's sake, you can't do that."

"But we have the rubber raft and oars and . . ." Annie's imagination knew no bounds.

"Annie, do you know what St. Bernard claws would do to a rubber raft? It would sink, sure as the world," Seth said, snatching two more slices of ham.

"Oh." Annie stopped talking for a moment. Then: "But if they're captains, they gotta hab a ship! Or it won't be real!"

"The boat doesn't have to be in the water to be a boat, does it?" Maggie asked.

Annie shook her head.

"Then Dad and his CO-CAPTAIN will stand in the boat on dry land." She said the word "co-captain" with very defined capital letters. "Everybody else can walk up the hallway, just like the aisle in church. How does that sound?"

Annie was smiling again. "Oh, boy. Dis is gonna be fun."

Fun?

I wondered. I looked across the room at Agatha. We had known each other such a short time . . . but . . .

Agatha Bliss and Judge Benjamin.

Hmmmmm.

Chapter 16

The next morning, the plans were set and reset a number of times.

It was to be an evening ceremony. By candlelight. Birthday candles.

Guess who thought of that?

Annie would be maid of honor; Maura, the flower girl.

We would enter through the hallway to the dining room so Maura could hold on to the wall.

Kathleen was to serve as mother of the bride and Seth was to usher.

No one had any idea whom he was going to usher, since it was a private ceremony and nobody else was invited.

Tom and Maggie were going to officiate.

What's more, Annie had all day to perfect her plans because Tom and Maggie and the rest of the family were going through closets and the garage in preparation for a church rummage sale.

Annie saw a television show once where the flower girl threw petals in front of the bride, so she spent the morning searching for roses.

Not a frequent find in winter.

I got a little nervous when she found a sharp pair of scissors. I followed her into the living room. Agatha was already there, dozing by the coffee table.

My, my.

Annie pruned the silk flower arrangement on the piano, took the baby's breath from the dry sink, and added live Schlefferra leaves for color.

You had to admire her creative zeal.

She found an old basket and decorated it with a drapery tieback.

Then there was the veil.

As far as I was concerned, Agatha didn't need anything to make herself beautiful, but Annie had other ideas.

Annie rummaged through the cedar closet and dug up a white veil.

I was not sure Maggie was going to love this.

Tom came up for a roll of paper towels just as Annie was sorting through his ties. She wanted to find the perfect one for the groom.

Why did that word rhyme with "doom"?

Annie had stopped at a horrid pink paisley tie that gave me a headache just thinking of the dyes it had absorbed.

"Annie?" Tom picked two silk ties off the floor. "You know you're not supposed to be in here without permission."

"But you said I could work on the weddin'," Annie said, "and Judge has to be spiffy, too."

"Well . . ." Tom hedged.

While he hesitated, Annie quickly tied the ugly tie around my neck. "See? Doesn't Judge look swell?"

Apparently Tom had the same reaction to the tie that I did. I'd never seen him wear it. He looked at me sympathetically.

"Look, if he must dress up," Tom said finally, "let's at least keep him formal."

Tom dug in his bottom drawer for the black satin bow tie that went with his old tuxedo. "I think this has the Judge's stamp on it."

He clipped it to my collar. "Better," he said,

looking at Annie but turning aside to wink at me.

Much better. Annie and I could both live with it.

I wondered if Agatha really wanted to do this. She hadn't been around kids all that much. Did it seem too crazy? And yet it seemed natural having her here.

When "wardrobe" had finished with me, I went looking for her.

She was sitting in the formal living room in front of the wall that held all the family pictures. There were baby pictures, Maggie and Tom's wedding pictures, pictures of me, pictures of family groupings—and on the floor, just in front of that wall, she had placed her stocking with its picture of her.

She looked up at me and I knew. She wanted to belong.

Kathleen and Seth helped in the kitchen, making meatballs, roast beef roll-ups with cream cheese and horseradish, and a chocolate cake for the "recepshun." The division of labor consisted of Kathleen's cooking and Seth's tasting.

Annie spent another hour making designs on napkins. They looked like keyholes, but I heard her say they were wedding bells.

Annie took one look at everyone after they had finished the Saturday chores and insisted that they change into dress-up clothes.

By five forty-five, the party began assembling.

Agatha stood still while Kathleen secured her veil with hairpins.

That had to be a good deal more uncomfortable than my tie.

The dining room table was pushed to one side, and I stood next to it. Tom and Maggie were in the boat that they had dragged from the pool area. They were barefoot, each holding matching address books with some words written down inside.

Seth "ushered" four teddy bears, a Barbie doll, a gray elephant with half a trunk, and a china sparrow into seats under the dining room table.

Seth pushed the button on the tape deck. He didn't own the wedding march, so he played the "Battle Hymn of the Republic," which he had taped a long time ago for the Boy Scouts.

The most difficult moment was when Seth realized he had to "usher" the mother of the bride, Kathleen, to her place.

He actually put his arm through Kathleen's arm without holding his nose.

Annie led the procession. She was wearing one

of Maggie's silk blouses and high heels. The paisley tie that was meant for me belted her outfit. It looked rather campy. Annie was going to be a trendsetter some day.

Maura wore a light blue kimono. It was the only thing she had that resembled a long skirt. It didn't do much to make walking easier. Besides, she carried the basket of flowers that Annie had assembled earlier, so she didn't have both hands free to hold on to the wall.

But she made it. All the way. She threw the silk petals, the baby's breath, the Schlefferra leaves, everything, yelling "Whoopeee!" right in the middle of the hall.

Annie gasped. It wasn't what she had planned but it would have to do. There was no turning back now.

Maggie looked rather puzzled by the silk petals, but she said nothing.

Then it was Agatha's turn.

Maggie very softly called "Come, Agatha," and she came.

I wanted to applaud.

She walked down that hallway with dignity and patience, looking like the beautiful St. Bernard that she was.

I knew why she went through with Annie's ceremony. It was because Agatha loved us, all of us.

Just as we loved her.

Agatha Bliss *belonged.*

Tom cleared his throat, Maggie nodded, and Annie put a *Shhh!* finger to her lips.

Annie's ceremony began.

I suddenly realized that it meant as much to me as it did to Annie.

It was over in minutes.

I heard the words, a little music, and some cheering.

Some flashbulbs popped. Then the family party began.

When it was over, Agatha and I both realized something important. It wasn't an ending. It was a beginning.

When the sun set on our very special day, Agatha and I walked out back together.

We sat beneath the apple trees quietly enjoying the dusk.

I looked at Agatha, her fine, friendly face, so serene, so pleasant.

Maggie called us when it was nearly ten o'-

clock. "Weatherman says it will be pretty cold tonight, you two," she announced. "Better sleep in."

We walked through the house before we settled down. It was *our* job now. We would share the duty of guarding the O'Riley family.

In the living room along the picture wall, Agatha paused.

Right next to the most recent family portrait, Maggie had hung Agatha's stocking. And right next to that was a *Polaroid* shot of two married St. Bernards. . . .

Thanks, Annie.